CHAPTER 1

Learn about:

- A deadly injection
- Suicide or murder?
- Studying word evidence

Table of Contents

Edge Books are published by Capstone Press,
151 Good Counsel Drive, P.O. Box 669, Mankato, Minnesota 56002.
www.capstonepress.com

Library of Congress Cataloging-in-Publication Data
Martin, Michael, 1948–
    Word evidence / by Michael Martin.
    p. cm.   (Edge books. Forensic crime solvers)
    Summary: "Describes how linguistic evidence is used to solve crimes"—Provided by
publisher.
    Includes bibliographical references and index.
    ISBN-13: 978-0-7368-6790-0 (hardcover)
    ISBN-10: 0-7368-6790-2 (hardcover)
    ISBN-13: 978-0-7368-7874-6 (softcover pbk.)
    ISBN-10: 0-7368-7874-2 (softcover pbk.)
    1. Forensic linguistics—Juvenile literature. I. Title. II. Series.
HV8073.5.M17 2007
363.25'65—dc22   2006024896

Editorial Credits
Angie Kaelberer, editor; Juliette Peters, set designer; Ted Williams, book designer;
    Wanda Winch, photo researcher/photo editor

Photo Credits
AP/Wide World Photos/Eric Draper, 24
Capstone Press/Karon Dubke, front cover, 4, 6, 7, 8, 10, 29
Corbis/Andrew Lichtenstein, 13; Bettmann, 17; Ralf-Finn Hestoft, 22;
    Reuters/Tami Chappell, 26
Getty Images Inc./AFP/Paul Sakuma, 20; Alex Wong, 28; Stephen J. Dubner, 23
iStockphoto Inc./Brad Denoon, 1
PhotoEdit Inc./Chris Smith, 14; Spencer Grant, 12, 18
Shutterstock, back cover; Menna, 16

Note: The case presented in Chapter 1 of this book is fictional.

1 2 3 4 5 6 12 11 10 09 08 07

Forensic Crime Solvers

Word Evidence

by **Michael Martin**

Consultant:
Robert A. Leonard, PhD
Professor of Linguistics and Director of the Forensic Linguistics Project
Chair, Department of Comparative Literature and Languages
Hofstra University, Hempstead, New York

Capstone *press* ®
Mankato, Minnesota

A Note from the Grave

Beth Johnson and Kelly Madison were roommates. One evening, the police received a frantic phone call from Kelly. She told an officer she came home from work to find Beth in her bed. She wasn't breathing. An ambulance raced to the house. Paramedics confirmed Beth was dead.

Crime scene investigators (CSIs) arrived soon after. As they searched the house for clues, they discovered nothing unusual. But an autopsy of Beth's body a few days later showed something troubling. Beth's blood contained small amounts of the deadly poison arsenic. There was a needle mark in her arm. An injection of the poison had killed Beth.

◀ Kelly called the police after finding Beth's body.

Who Killed Beth?

When the police questioned Kelly, she told them Beth had been unhappy for several weeks. She showed them a message she said she found on Beth's computer. It was a suicide note. The officers were suspicious. They wondered if Beth had really killed herself. Or had Kelly injected Beth with the arsenic and then wrote the note to cover her tracks? The case depended on who actually wrote the note.

The police called in forensic linguist Denise Greer for help. Forensic linguists are experts in how language is used. They analyze messages in criminal cases.

Kelly told the police that Beth had killed herself.

Greer looked for similarities between the suicide note and Beth's e-mails.

Word by Word

Greer compared the wording in some of Beth's other e-mails to the note. She also compared the note to messages Kelly had written. She looked closely at how the words and sentences were put together. Greer also reviewed the words themselves. She even looked at the spelling and punctuation.

Beth had never been a good student. She had dropped out of high school when she was 16. And she didn't have a large vocabulary. Yet the note contained words like "towering" and "burden." These were words no one had ever heard Beth use.

Catching a Killer

After careful study, Greer determined Beth probably hadn't written the note. Her findings increased officers' suspicions about Kelly. They learned that Kelly was interested in Beth's boyfriend. Plus, Beth's friends told them that she hadn't seemed unhappy.

The police questioned Kelly again. After two hours, Kelly broke down in tears. She told the officers that she and Beth had a fight. Beth said she was moving out and never wanted to see Kelly again. Kelly said she injected the poison into Beth's arm after Beth fell asleep that night. Kelly wrote the suicide note to mislead the police. Instead, her own words helped convict her of murder.

◄ Kelly was arrested and booked at the police station.

CHAPTER 2

3 1833 05230 8761

Learn about:
- Forms of communication
- Speech patterns
- Sentence structure

Hidden Patterns

Forensic linguists catch criminals by studying how they use words. The words might be in a bomb threat left on a telephone answering machine. Or they could be part of an e-mail or a letter.

Letters or notes can reveal far more about their writers than people realize. One person might use the word "excellent" to describe something good. Another might use the word "cool." The difference could be a clue to a person's age. Young people are more likely to use slang words.

◀ Forensic linguists sometimes use computers to listen to audio messages.

People who learn English as a second language use different speech patterns than native speakers do.

Rhythms of Speech

Phonology is the study of speech sound patterns. Everyone tends to use certain patterns when they speak or write messages. They usually aren't aware of these patterns.

The way people pronounce words can depend on the area where they live. In Boston, Massachusetts, some people pronounce the word "car" as "cah." A person from Canada might pronounce "about" in a way that makes it sound like "a boat" to Americans.

Urban areas like New York City are home to many languages and accents.

Building Blocks of Language

The study of how words are put together is called morphology. People's backgrounds can affect how they put words together and the phrases they use. Forensic linguists study the structure of entire sentences, which is called syntax. They also study semantics, or the meanings of words.

Semantics and syntax can change over time and from place to place. In the early 1800s, the word "broadcast" meant to scatter seeds over the ground. Today, people use this word to refer to signals sent by radio and TV.

Also, a person from England might form sentences much differently than someone from the United States. The English person might ask, "Will you be joining us for dinner this evening?" The American might say, "Are you coming by for supper tonight?"

After forensic linguists find the patterns in a message, they are ready for the next step. They might be asked to compare one message to another to see if the patterns are alike. Police may want to know whether the same person could have written both messages.

◄ The way English people speak can seem formal to Americans.

Finding a Suspect

At times, police don't have a sample of a suspect's communication. Sometimes, they don't even have a suspect. Even then, forensic linguists can help.

Serial killers are murderers who kill again and again. They sometimes write letters to the police or to newspapers. They tend to brag about how no one can catch them.

Preventing a Mistake

Forensic linguists don't just help catch criminals. Sometimes they stop investigations from heading in the wrong direction. In 1987, Pan American Airlines in Los Angeles received a number of bomb threats by phone. The caller seemed to Californians to have a New York accent. Police arrested an airline employee from New York because his voice sounded like the voice in the threats.

But then linguist William Labov listened to the tapes. Right away, he realized something was wrong. The accent on the tapes was not a New York accent after all. It was actually a Boston accent. The employee was released and the search for the real criminal continued.

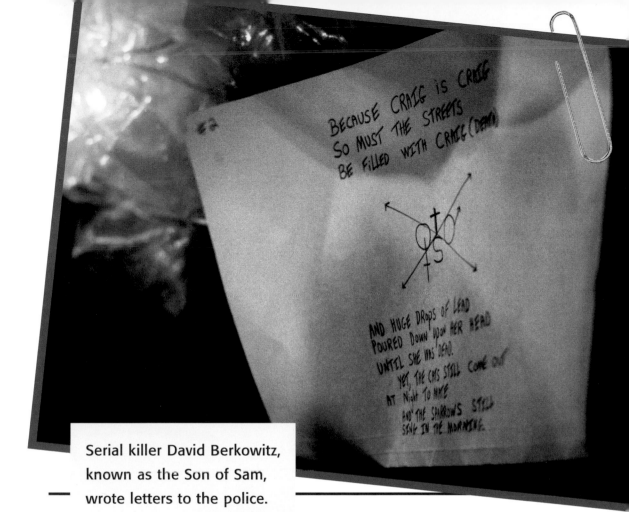

Serial killer David Berkowitz, known as the Son of Sam, wrote letters to the police.

Forensic linguists study these letters and other written or spoken evidence for clues. They can usually tell how much education the writer or speaker has. Slang or unusual phrases can also hint at the writer or speaker's background. So can dozens of other language characteristics. Such information saves time by helping police narrow the group of possible suspects.

CHAPTER 3

Learn about:

- Conversational analysis
- Computers
- The Unabomber

Cracking the Case

On a new case, linguists first look at the type of evidence. The evidence might be a tape-recorded message or conversation. It could be a handwritten note or an e-mail message. Linguists use the form of the message to decide which language tools will work best.

A Question of Communication

One language tool is called conversational analysis. It is used for both spoken and written communication between two or more people.

Police who are questioning suspects often record the conversations. Sometimes, the questioning ends with the suspects confessing. Later on, suspects may claim they didn't understand what was happening, especially if they don't speak English well. They may say they were tricked into signing a confession.

◄ Word evidence is especially important when questioning suspects.

Forensic linguists are sometimes asked to determine if a confession is real. They study the recorded conversation to see if the suspect's responses show true understanding. If the suspect misunderstood the questions, lawyers might not be able to use the confession in court.

David Kaczynski (below) became suspicious that his brother, Ted, was the Unabomber.

Tracking the Unabomber

Forensic linguists also use computers. Computers helped convict a killer nicknamed the Unabomber. This person sent bombs through the mail. The bombs killed three people and wounded 29 others.

In 1995, the Unabomber typed a 35,000-word essay that he sent to the *New York Times* and the *Washington Post.* He said he would stop the bombings if the newspapers printed the essay. Both newspapers published the essay on September 19, 1995.

A man named David Kaczynski read the essay. He thought the Unabomber's writing style sounded like that of his older brother, Ted. David contacted the police, but they needed legal permission to search Ted's home. Investigators loaded the essay and some of Ted's writings into a computer database. The database helped a team of forensic linguists compare the essay to Ted's work. They seemed to match. A judge then ruled that Ted's house could be searched. Inside, the police found other writings and materials for making bombs.

Police arrested Ted Kaczynski in Montana in 1996.

Language Clues

At the trial, linguist Don Foster spoke about an unusual phrase found in the Unabomber's writings. Foster used a computer to search through 290,000 works of English literature. The computer found 200 examples of the odd phrase. All of them were from British works.

The British spell certain words differently than Americans do. Even though he was not British, Kaczynski sometimes used British spelling. For example, instead of "license," he often wrote "licence." The linguist's findings supported the fact that Kaczynski and the Unabomber were the same person. Kaczynski was sentenced to life in prison.

Ted Kaczynski is serving his sentence at the supermax prison in Florence, Colorado.

CHAPTER 4

Learn about:

- 1996 Olympic bombings
- Communication clues
- An anonymous writer

Caught in a Web of Words

Forensic linguists rarely solve crimes by themselves. But their findings often lead police to a suspect. A good example is the 1996 bombing at the Olympic Games in Atlanta, Georgia. The explosion killed one person and wounded 111 others.

Other bombings occurred in Alabama and Georgia around the same time. The police didn't realize they were the work of the same person at first. But letters sent to newspapers and television stations after each bombing were suspiciously alike. They were printed in large block letters. The printing made it impossible for the Federal Bureau of Investigation (FBI) to do a handwriting analysis.

◀ On July 27, 1996, a bomb exploded in Centennial Park in Atlanta.

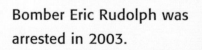

Bomber Eric Rudolph was arrested in 2003.

Same Structure

The FBI took the messages to a forensic linguist. By this time, they had a long list of suspects. One of them, Eric Rudolph, fled before anyone could question him.

The linguist compared the printed messages with known samples of Rudolph's writing. He found similarities in spelling and punctuation and even in the spaces left between certain letters. The linguist concluded that Rudolph had written the letters. In 2003, Rudolph was captured and pled guilty to the bombings.

Uncovering Secrets

Word evidence is becoming more important to police as people communicate less with handwritten messages. Phone calls, e-mails, and documents printed from computers make it easier for communicators to hide who they are.

Forensic linguistics helped prove that Joe Klein (above) wrote *Primary Colors.*

Yet, forensic linguists can still uncover important clues in computer and phone messages. No matter how hard criminals try to disguise their actions, they must use language. And the words they choose will give them away.

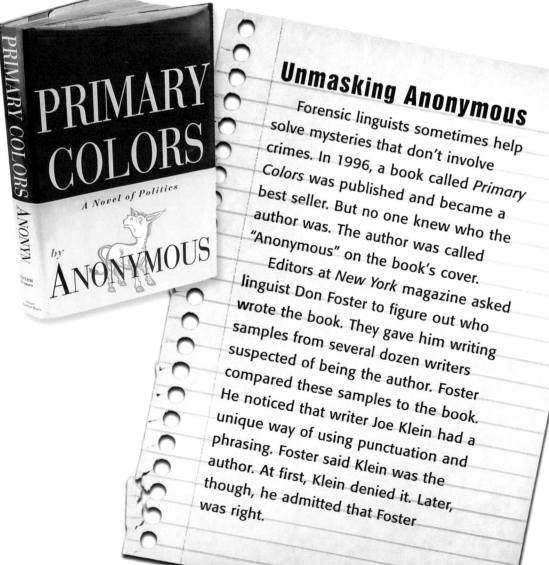

Unmasking Anonymous

Forensic linguists sometimes help solve mysteries that don't involve crimes. In 1996, a book called *Primary Colors* was published and became a best seller. But no one knew who the author was. The author was called "Anonymous" on the book's cover. Editors at *New York* magazine asked linguist Don Foster to figure out who wrote the book. They gave him writing samples from several dozen writers suspected of being the author. Foster compared these samples to the book. He noticed that writer Joe Klein had a unique way of using punctuation and phrasing. Foster said Klein was the author. At first, Klein denied it. Later, though, he admitted that Foster was right.

Glossary

arsenic (AR-suh-nik)—a poisonous chemical

autopsy (AW-top-see)—an examination performed on a dead body to find the cause of death

linguistics (lin-GWIS-tiks)—the study of language

morphology (mor-FAH-luh-jee)—the study of the patterns of word formation in a language

paramedic (pa-ruh-MEH-dik)—a person who treats sick and hurt people; paramedics travel in ambulances to places where people need treatment.

phonology (fuh-NAH-luh-jee)—the study of the patterns of speech sounds in a language

semantics (si-MAN-tiks)—the study of word meanings

syntax (SIN-taks)—the study of the way words are put together to make phrases and sentences

Read More

Mattern, Joanne. *Forensics.* Science on the Edge. San Diego: Blackbirch Press, 2004.

Stewart, Gail. *Forensics.* Lucent Library of Science and Technology. Farmington Hills, Mich.: Lucent Books, 2006.

Thornburg, Linda. *Cool Careers for Girls as Crime Solvers.* Manassas Park, Va.: Impact Publications, 2002.

Internet Sites

FactHound offers a safe, fun way to find Internet sites related to this book. All of the sites on FactHound have been researched by our staff.

Here's how:

1. Visit *www.facthound.com*

2. Choose your grade level.

3. Type in this book ID **0736867902** for age-appropriate sites. You may also browse subjects by clicking on letters, or by clicking on pictures and words.

4. Click on the **Fetch It** button.

FactHound will fetch the best sites for you!

Index